Ming Ling

Written by Stephen Cosgrove
Illustrated by Robin James

A Serendipity™ Book

PRICE STERN SLOAN
Los Angeles

The Serendipity™ Series was created by Stephen Cosgrove and Robin James.

Copyright © 1995, 1978 Price Stern Sloan, Inc.
Published by Price Stern Sloan, Inc.,
• A member of The Putnam & Grosset Group, New York, New York.

Printed in the United States of America. Published simultaneously in Canada.
All rights reserved. No part of this publication may be reproduced, stored in a retrieval system,
or transmitted, in any form or by any means, electronic, mechanical, photocopying, recording,
or otherwise, without the prior written permission of the publisher.

Library of Congress Catalog Card Number: 95-68375

ISBN 0-8431-3922-6

Serendipity™ and The Pink Dragon® are trademarks of Price Stern Sloan, Inc.

First Revised Edition
1 3 5 7 9 10 8 6 4 2

Dedicated to William Russe and all the pandas of the world. May they all live forever in the magical Panda Pines.

—*Stephen*

West of west and east of east lay the forest called the Panda Pines. Because of the gentle rains, plants grew in great profusion there. Brilliant flowers and bamboo thickets shimmered in the magical mists surrounding the Panda Pines.

As you can well imagine, this forest of bamboo provided a marvelous shelter for feathered birds of every kind, including cockatiels and cockatoos—and even a pair of parrots. All would flutter above and about the thicket, chattering their melodic songs.

Other than the birds, the only creature that lived there was a grumbly panda named Ming Ling. Ming Ling had two passions in life, to eat and to sleep. She wasn't grouchy by nature, but the birds of the thicket often ate her food and robbed her of her rest.

The birds would eat all of Ming Ling's pine nuts, her favorite thing to eat. Then they would sit in the trees after they ate, singing with puffed feathery chests. This would wake and frustrate the hungry panda even more.

One special morning when it would have felt good to sleep another hour or two, the birds started making a loud racket by singing and flapping their wings against the bamboo leaves. With a "Ruff!" and a "Whuff!" Ming Ling woke up abruptly.

"Why can't they wake up when I wake up?" she grumbled as she rubbed the sleep from her eyes. "What I need is a bird who will talk when I talk, walk when I walk, and most of all, sleep when I sleep!" With that she sat on her haunches and roared into the trees, scaring a bird or two. Ming Ling knew she was going to have another really bad day.

Because she couldn't sleep as long as she wanted to or eat all that she wished, Ming Ling became more and more cranky. She stomped around and grumbled looking for pine nuts. In a furious rage she grabbed some branches in her mighty paws, shaking them like a whip in the wind.

Whenever Ming Ling was in a cranky mood, the birds would start to sing a happy song. But she was so surly that she began chasing and snapping at them with her teeth. She never caught one—and probably wouldn't know what to do if she did—but a bird's happy fluttering turned into frightened flittering, and a few feathers graced the corners of Ming Ling's mouth as the bird escaped.

One day all the birds, including the cockatiels and cockatoos, decided they could stand it no more. They packed up their nests and flew away. The silence that followed was like a golden blanket to Ming Ling, who wrapped herself in the delicious hush. Peacefully she ate tender bamboo shoots and leaves. It was so absolutely still that she almost started to giggle, but that would have broken the warm, gentle stillness of the day.

It was so perfectly quiet that after she ate her fill she curled into a soft furry ball and, with no one or no bird to distract her, fell fast asleep.

Minutes turned to hours, hours turned to days, days turned to weeks. Suddenly the peace and quiet of the thicket began to press on Ming Ling's ears. Just as the birds had made too much noise for her, the silence hung heavy on her shoulders.

She wandered throughout Panda Pines searching for even one bird, but none could be found. At long last when Ming Ling was about to give up, she spied a rather plump, red parrot sitting on a bamboo branch. She looked at the parrot as it looked at her—and neither spoke a word.

Finally Ming Ling could take the silence no more and eagerly said, "Do you speak?"

The parrot cocked its head to one side and said, "Do you speak?"

Ming Ling slowly scratched her head and said, "Well, of course . . . but do *you* speak?"

The parrot paced from one end of the branch to the other and said, "Well, of course . . . but do *you* speak?"

Ming Ling growled, "You're being silly!"

Then the parrot growled, "You're being silly!"

Ming Ling's eyes opened wide with amazement. She had found the perfect bird: a bird who would sleep when she slept and talk when she talked and say the words she loved to hear—her own.

This is great, Ming Ling thought to herself. This is my kind of bird! She began to walk slowly around the tree as the parrot mimicked her every move. "Pandas are great!" Ming Ling snickered out loud.

The parrot snickered back, "Pandas are great!"

"And Ming Ling is the greatest!" she laughed into her furry paw.

"And Ming Ling is the greatest!" the parrot laughed into its feathered wing.

With a smile as wide as the Panda Pines, Ming Ling giggled her way into the forest, with the parrot waddling behind.

The next day, after the sun had been up for about an hour, Ming Ling stretched in the warm leaves that were her nest. "What a gorgeous morning," she yawned.

Above her head she heard feathers rustle and a squawking voice yawned right back, "What a gorgeous morning."

So it went from day to day with Ming Ling talking and the parrot repeating her every word.

As the days wore on, Ming Ling became a little upset about their conversations. Though they talked throughout the day, it didn't seem that the parrot was adding anything. Finally one afternoon as Ming Ling drank from the stream (as usual the parrot was doing the same), the panda shouted loudly, "You dumb creature! Why don't you climb a tree and sing, or something?"

The parrot, its feathers ruffled, shouted just as loudly, "You dumb creature! Why don't you climb a tree and sing, or something?"

Ming Ling's eyes widened in anger and she screamed, "If you repeat what I say one more time, I'll eat you for dessert!"

For the first time in a long time the parrot didn't repeat her statement. The air was thick with silence.

The parrot fluttered up into a tree and looked down at the angry, confused panda. "What do you want, panda? First you want silence, then you don't, but now you do."

Sheepishly Ming Ling sat and gazed at the ground. "I don't know. I thought I wanted it quiet, but that was boring. Then I thought I wanted to hear someone talk when I talked, and now I don't know what I want." She paused, deep in thought. "Maybe if the birds all came back . . . "

"Well," said the parrot, "they'll never come back if you're going to roar at them!"

"Yes, but they make so much noise, and I need a lot of sleep!"

"Hmmm." The parrot paced on a branch, thinking out loud. "With a bit of cooperation and a pinch of compromise I think you both can survive."

From that day forward, whenever Ming Ling wished for silence she did nothing more than stuff bamboo leaves in her ears. The birds were so happy singing without interruption that they carried great piles of pine nuts and the most tender leaves for her to eat when she woke from her afternoon naps.

And sometimes, when Ming Ling wasn't looking and couldn't hear, the plump, red parrot mimicked her every word.

IF YOU LIVE IN A FOREST

AND DON'T KNOW HOW TO SHARE IT,

REMEMBER A PANDA NAMED MING LING

AND A VERY SILLY PARROT.

Serendipity™ Books

Created by
Stephen Cosgrove and Robin James

Enjoy all the delightful books in the Serendipity™ Series:

The above books, and many others, can be bought wherever books are sold.

PRICE STERN SLOAN
L o s   A n g e l e s